Amelia Bedelia

Goes Wild!

#4

☆ Amelia Bedelia

Goes Wild! ☆

MY ZOO

by Herman Parish

pictures by Lynne Avril

☆

me

 Greenwillow Books

An Imprint of HarperCollins Publishers

Library of Congress Cataloging-in-Publication Data
Parish, Herman.
Amelia Bedelia goes wild! / by Herman Parish ; pictures by Lynne Avril.
pages cm.—(Amelia Bedelia chapter books ; #4)
Summary: "Amelia Bedelia is sick the day her class goes to visit the zoo. She doesn't want to be left out,
so she comes up with a brilliant idea—she'll create a zoo in her backyard, using all her classmates' pets.
But she doesn't know exactly how to tell her parents about her great plan"—Provided by publisher.
ISBN 978-0-06-209507-7 (hardback)—ISBN 978-0-06-209506-0 (pbk. ed.)—ISBN 978-0-06-227058-0 (pob)
[1. Zoos—Fiction. 2. Animals—Fiction. 3. Humorous stories.] I. Avril, Lynne, (date) illustrator. II. Title.
PZ7.P2185Aoj 2014 [Fic]—dc23 2013035257

14 15 16 17 CG/RRDH 10 9 8 7 6 5 4 3 2 1 First Edition

 Greenwillow Books

Contents

Chapter 1

Sick as a ~~Dog~~ Finally

Amelia Bedelia was sick. She was really, really, really, really, *really* sick. She was sick of being in her bedroom. She was sick of playing with her animals and dolls.

1

She was sick of watching nature programs on TV. She was sick of gazing out the window at the beautiful spring day. She was sick of thinking about how much fun her class was having without her on the field trip to the zoo. Most of all, she was sick of being sick.

"How's the worst patient in the world?" asked Amelia Bedelia's mother. She put a bowl of soup and a grilled cheese sandwich on Amelia Bedelia's desk, along with Amelia Bedelia's favorite fruit, a banana.

Amelia Bedelia stood up in bed.

"I'm all better now!" she announced. To prove it, she jumped up and started

2

waving her arms around. Quickly she
plopped back down again.

"Mommy," she said, "make the room
stop spinning!"

"Don't make yourself dizzy,
sweetie," her mother said,
tucking her back in. "I don't
want you to fall and hit

your head, on top of having the flu!"

Amelia Bedelia began coughing.

"Are you okay?" asked her mother. "This pesky flu is one tough bug!"

"Flu comes from an insect?" said Amelia Bedelia. "That's gross! It's not fair that a tiny bug stopped me from going to the zoo. I'm missing all the cool animals!"

Only one good thing had happened while Amelia Bedelia was sick. She had gotten to watch a television show about monkeys, and she learned an amazing thing. Since monkeys eat lots of bananas, they have figured out a fast way to peel them. Instead of starting at the hard stalk at the top, they turn the banana upside down. Then they pinch the little nub at

Monkey Method for eating a BANANA!!!

1. Turn banana upside down.

2. Squeeze the smaller end

3. POP and PEEL!

the bottom, and the skin falls right off!

Amelia Bedelia peeled her banana the way she had seen the monkeys do it on TV. Presto! It worked! The skin fell right off. Amelia Bedelia ate her banana, but she didn't touch anything else. She was too sick!

Chapter 2

Not a Fit Night for Amelia Bedelia or Beast

When Amelia Bedelia's father got home from work, he sat on Amelia Bedelia's bed and began polishing off her sandwich and soup.

"Still sick as a dog, huh?" he asked. He looked around Amelia Bedelia's bedroom. "Hey, speaking of dogs, where's Finally?"

Amelia Bedelia was about to sneeze, so she pointed to her dog, who was curled up on a dog bed in the corner of her room.

"Ah-ah-AHHHH . . . CHOO!"

Ah-ah-AHHH...CHOO!

"*Choo!*" sneezed Finally, at exactly the same time.

"That's a neat trick," said her father. "So is Finally as sick as a dog too?"

"She has no choice," said Amelia Bedelia. "Finally is a dog. She can't be as sick as an elephant."

"Good point," said her dad. "Hey, you aren't playing possum, are you? You didn't miss your trip to the zoo on purpose."

"Daddy, what are you talking about?" asked Amelia Bedelia. "If I was a possum, I'd have my own cage at the zoo."

Amelia Bedelia's mother came in just as her father was swallowing the last bite of grilled cheese. "Oh, Amelia Bedelia," she said. "I'm glad you managed to eat your sandwich. You need to get your strength back."

Amelia Bedelia's father put his finger to his lips to signal that what had happened to her sandwich would be their secret. "I need my strength too," he said. "It's a jungle out there!

My office is a total zoo. It was wild today!"

"Sorry, honey," said Amelia Bedelia's mother. "Come tell me all about it in the kitchen, so Amelia Bedelia can rest."

"I almost forgot . . . little possum!" said Amelia Bedelia's father from the doorway. "Did you hear what happened today? A monkey escaped from the zoo! Maybe it's a good thing you stayed home. They might have mistaken you for him. We'd be sneaking into the zoo right this minute to rescue you!"

Usually Amelia Bedelia's father's jokes made her laugh. This was not one of those times, though. She *really* was sick!

Amelia Bedelia's mother rolled her eyes. "Come along, honey," she said. "I need help with dinner."

Amelia Bedelia buried her face in her pillow. She was sick, and now she was

heartsick too. This disaster was getting worse. Not only had she missed the thrill of being at the zoo on an amazing field trip, but a monkey had escaped while her class was there! That would never, ever happen again. What if she

had been able to capture it? What if—
wha . . . whaaa-CHOO!

Amelia Bedelia felt more miserable than ever. The only thing she'd caught was a bug—the flu. She burrowed under her blankets like a hibernating bear. It was getting windy outside. Thunder was rumbling closer. Tree branches clattered against her window. They sounded like claws tapping and scratching. Her dad was right. It *was* a jungle out there! Lightning flashed and thunder roared. Or was that an enormous lightning bug and a lion? Amelia Bedelia tossed and turned. She felt hot, then cold. Strange pictures popped into her head.

Her stuffed animals were on the move. A penguin waddled behind a koala riding a hippopotamus. The animals gathered in a circle on her bedspread, drinking from a water hole at her feet.

Suddenly she was in her backyard. The sky was filled with enormous puffy clouds shaped like flamingoes. A giant bunny and an otter peeked out from behind her mom's azaleas. A giraffe was nibbling on their garage. Then her class came walking by.

Amelia Bedelia was so glad to see everyone.

"How was the zoo?" she asked.

"The zoo was nice," said her friend Clay. "But your backyard is way better. Help us look for the missing monkey!"

Amelia Bedelia and her classmates searched everywhere, and she introduced them to all of her animals.

"Do you feel better, pretty pup?" said Amelia Bedelia when she spotted Finally next to the birdbath.

"I'm fine now," said Finally. "But for a while, I was as sick as Amelia Bedelia!"

Amelia Bedelia couldn't believe that her dog was actually talking! Her cheeks burned hotter and hotter and her head pounded . . . until, at last, her fever broke. She listened to the rain gently drumming on her window and fell asleep.

The next morning, as soon as Amelia Bedelia woke up, she had the strangest idea of her life. It was a really Big Idea. She wanted to go to school right away and tell her friends (even though it was Saturday). She needed their help. Amelia Bedelia was certain that when they heard her Big Idea, they would be as excited as she was. They might think it was weird or even wacky. But one thing was certain . . . it was going to be *wild*.

Chapter 3

Heard Instinct

By Monday, Amelia Bedelia had beaten her flu bug and was back in school. She couldn't wait to tell everyone about her Big Idea. But her classmates were still talking and laughing about their super-fun field trip. She felt bad—not sick, just left out.

"Class!" called out their teacher,

Mrs. Shauk. She had long, pointy fingernails painted shiny red. Her nickname was "the Hawk," because she saw everything, even with her back turned. "Settle down, please," she said.

Feeling the gaze of the Hawk upon her, Amelia Bedelia sat up straighter.

"Amelia Bedelia," said Mrs. Shauk, "we're glad you are feeling better. We really missed you on the field trip, so we got you a souvenir from the gift shop."

Suzanne presented Amelia Bedelia with a box decorated with

pictures of animals. Everyone gathered around Amelia Bedelia's desk as she opened it. Staring up at her from the tissue paper was the cutest plush monkey she'd ever seen! The gift made her feel a lot better. She gave the monkey a big hug and Suzanne a bigger hug. "Thanks for thinking of me," she said to everyone.

"It's a life-size squirrel monkey," said Suzanne. "That's the same kind that escaped from the zoo. It ran right by us!"

"I thought it was a baby," said Chip.

"I thought it was you," said Daisy.

"Oook-oook-chaboook!" chirped Chip.

Everyone burst out laughing. Mrs. Shauk clapped three times to restore order.

"Amelia Bedelia," she said, "we have other exciting things to share with you. Before the trip, you were each assigned an animal to investigate. And now that you've seen the real thing, I want each of you to write a report about your animal. You can add pictures if you'd like, and be prepared to present your

19

research to the class this afternoon."

Amelia Bedelia had chosen monkeys as her animal. But she wondered how she was going to write her report if she hadn't seen a real one at the zoo. Staring at the stuffed squirrel monkey perched on her desk, Amelia Bedelia got an idea. She would take the banana her mom had packed in her lunch box and show everyone how a monkey would peel it. She would be presenting something she'd seen a monkey do, even if it was only on TV.

"Feel free to share your writing with

one another," Mrs. Shauk said. "Make suggestions and helpful comments. But please, no reading aloud."

No reading allowed? That made no sense to Amelia Bedelia. "If there's no reading allowed," she asked, "how will we know what anyone else wrote?"

"You're allowed to read, but not aloud," said Mrs. Shauk.

Amelia Bedelia wished Mrs. Shauk would make up her mind. Was reading allowed or not allowed?

"Can I read or not?" she asked.

"Of course," said Mrs. Shauk. "I just need to be able to hear myself think."

Amelia Bedelia was even more confused. She'd never, ever heard herself

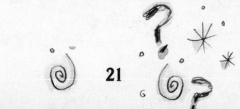

think, and now reading was not allowed. Amelia Bedelia hadn't missed *that* many days of school, had she?

She felt lost and began wishing she had the flu again so she could go home. Amelia Bedelia got up to get her banana from her cubby so she could work on her report.

"Where are you going?" asked Mrs. Shauk.

"I need my banana for writing," said Amelia Bedelia.

"Use your pencil, please," said Mrs. Shauk. "It writes better than a banana."

Everyone giggled as Amelia Bedelia sat

back down. Now she couldn't even write about peeling a banana. What should she do?

Aha! thought Amelia Bedelia. She would write about her Big Idea.

After lunch, everyone presented their reports. Amelia Bedelia learned many interesting facts about the animals at the zoo. When it was her turn, Amelia Bedelia stood up and read.

My Zoo
by Amelia Bedelia

I was too sick to go to the zoo. I was very sad. So I set up my stuffed animals like they were in the zoo. I visited them in my room. That night, I dreamed there were animals in my backyard. There were all kinds of creatures, normal ones and weird ones. I dreamed that you all came to see them. Some of the animals ~~where~~ were your pets, but dressed up like they were wild. That is why I have decided to make a zoo in my backyard. Come over to my house after school and help me plan what it will look like and what animals will be in it. Bring your pets too, if you would like them to be in my zoo.

Amelia Bedelia sat down. The room was completely quiet. She picked up her squirrel monkey and tickled its ears. Did they think her report was dumb?

Finally Clay whistled. "That would be wild, Amelia Bedelia," he said.

"I hope so," said Amelia Bedelia. "That's my plan."

Clap

Yay!

Hooray!

Clap

Clap

!!

Amelia Bedelia had forgotten the best
part, so she stood up again and added,
"If you come over, I'll show you how a
monkey eats a banana. It's really cool."

Everyone cheered.

Cla

"Our field trip to the zoo isn't over
yet," said Teddy. "It's just moved to
Amelia Bedelia's backyard!"

Clap
Clap!

Clap

Yay!

Chapter 4

Dog + Pony Show

(and snakes and mice and everything else)

As usual, Amelia Bedelia rode the bus home. And as usual, her mother was waiting for her at the bus stop.

"Mom," said Amelia Bedelia, "do we have lots of bananas, like maybe a ton of bananas?"

"Of course, sweetie," said her mother. "They're your favorite."

"Good. Because we might need them." As they walked home, Amelia Bedelia explained to her mother that, right at that moment, almost her entire class was asking permission to come over to Amelia Bedelia's house to work on a zoo project.

"Is it okay?" she asked. "Please? We'll stay in the yard and we won't mess anything up."

"Sounds like a Big Idea to me," said Amelia Bedelia's mother. "I'll make some calls. I bet we can make it work." She set two large bunches of bananas on the kitchen table. "Here you go."

"Thanks, Mom!" Amelia Bedelia gave

her mother a big hug, grabbed the bananas, and headed outside with a notebook and pencil. She put the bananas on the patio table and drew a map of her backyard. She labeled it MY BACKYARD, B.Z. (BEFORE ZOO). This map showed her what she had to work with and how to put things back where they belonged when her project was over. She even made a key.

Once Amelia Bedelia figured out what she wanted, she would make another drawing called MY BACKYARD, A.Z. (AFTER ZOO).

key

= swing set
= berry bush
= azalea bush

= picnic table
= bird bath and garden

= apple tree
= fountain and fish pond
= big tree with rope swing

My Backyard, B.Z. (Before Zoo)

Garage

back door

my room (upstairs)

← H O U S E →

FRONT DOOR

Mrs. Adams's house

The kids from Amelia Bedelia's class started showing up one by one. Everyone went out back. Amelia Bedelia walked around her yard with her friends, investigating the possibilities. She got so many good ideas. For example, Skip loved her rope swing. He gave her an idea each time he swung by.

"Make this swing . . .

. . . part of the zoo. . . .

. . . You swing into the zoo . . .

. . . like an explorer. . . .

. . . There should be water . . .

. . . a pool of water . . .

. . . you have to swing over . . .

. . . to get into the zoo!"

Amelia Bedelia wrote everything down in her notebook. "I've got a wading pool," she said. "I'll fill it up and put it underneath the swing."

"Perfect," said Skip. Then he yelled like an ape-man. *"Ahhh-y-ahhh-yeeeeh-ohhhh!!!"*

Ahhh-y-ahh-yeeeeh-ohhhh!!!

Amelia Bedelia's mother ran outside carrying a first-aid kit. "Who got hurt? Where's the patient?"

Skip was embarrassed to say that he had yelled just for fun. Amelia Bedelia was embarrassed that her mom was acting like she worked in the emergency room. "Mom," she said, "no one is hurt. And no one is going to get hurt!"

A few minutes later, Angel was dropped off by her babysitter. She was carrying a really big cage. She set it down on the patio and whipped off the cloth covering.

"Whoa!" said Clay. "Is that a python?"

"Yup," said Angel. "It's a ball python. Her name is Squeezer."

Amelia Bedelia couldn't believe that Angel actually had a snake for a pet! As Squeezer coiled and uncoiled and slithered around the cage, Angel explained how she cared for her. "She only moves around when she's hungry," she said. "And she's nocturnal. That

means she's active at night and mostly sleeps during the day."

"Squeezer will be the star of the zoo," said Amelia Bedelia. "That's for sure!"

Everyone brought an animal or an interesting animal display. Roger brought a deer's head mounted on a plaque. The deer had big antlers. "This is a trophy buck," he said. "We keep it in our family room."

"Where's the rest of it?" asked Amelia Bedelia.

"We ate it," said Roger.

Amelia Bedelia didn't know what to say about that, but she knew that Roger's dad probably wouldn't be thrilled to have his prized deer displayed in a backyard zoo. She told Roger that live animals were more exciting than parts of a dead one, so he went home to find something else.

Penny arrived wearing a white mouse on her shoulder. "Meet Oswald," she said. "He'd love to be in your zoo."

Oswald was the cutest mouse Amelia Bedelia had ever seen! His tiny ears were adorable, and his eyes were sparkly brown. This zoo was going to be fantastic!

Amelia Bedelia spent the rest of the afternoon meeting gerbils, hamsters, chinchillas, and rabbits, and making lists

of ideas in her notebook . . . until there was a problem . . . a long slithering problem.

"Where's Oswald?" yelled Penny. "My mouse is missing! Oswald? Oswald!"

Everyone searched the yard for Oswald.

They looked absolutely everywhere, but there was no sign of the little white mouse.

"Check out Angel's snake," whispered Clay to Amelia Bedelia. "It was moving around a lot because it was hungry. Now it's snoozing."

Amelia Bedelia looked at Squeezer. The python was coiled up, taking a nap. Amelia Bedelia shivered.

"Oswald? Oswald!" cried Penny. "Come here, baby mouse!"

"Squeezer doesn't look that hungry anymore," whispered Clay. "I think Oswald was lunch!"

Amelia Bedelia felt like screaming.

"*Eeeeeeeeeeeeeeeeeeeeeeeeeeekkkkkk!*"
came a cry from the kitchen. Amelia
Bedelia's mother dashed outside.

"Never mind," said Clay. "I think we
found Oswald."

Penny coaxed her mouse from under
the refrigerator with a morsel of cheddar.

"Don't worry, Oswald is fine," she
said. "You just scared him."

"What a relief," said Amelia Bedelia's mother, though she didn't sound relieved. She was staring straight at Amelia Bedelia, who knew that she would hear about this after her friends left.

That night, Amelia Bedelia was sent to bed early. She wasn't being punished.

Her mother just wanted to make sure her bug didn't come back. Amelia Bedelia perched her new plush monkey on her windowsill so it could look out at the backyard zoo. She imagined all the fantastic displays and games she would create. She fell asleep dreaming about how great her zoo was going to be.

Chapter 5

The Best-Laid Plans of Mice and Amelia Bedelia

The next morning was bright and sunny. Amelia Bedelia's father had to leave for work earlier than usual for an important meeting. He kissed Amelia Bedelia and her mother good-bye and ran out the door. In less than a minute he was back, soaked from head to toe.

"Did you forget your umbrella?"

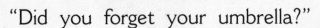

42

asked Amelia Bedelia.

"It's sunny—I don't need an umbrella!" said her father, fuming. "I need answers. Who left a pile of banana peels in front of the door to the garage?"

Amelia Bedelia's mother looked right at her. "What did you do with those bananas I gave you yesterday?" she asked.

"Nothing," said Amelia Bedelia. "I was going to show my friends how a monkey peels a banana, but we ran out of time. I left the bananas on the patio table. Sorry!"

"Well, somebody ate them!" said her father. "I slipped on those peels and went flying."

"Oh, honey, are you hurt?" asked Amelia Bedelia's mother.

"I don't think so," said her father. "Luckily I landed in a wading pool full of water. It broke my fall."

"That was lucky," said Amelia Bedelia. It was even luckier that it was time to catch the school bus.

Amelia Bedelia kissed her mom and dad good-bye, grabbed her backpack, and raced out the kitchen door. She took a quick detour and looked at the banana peels. *That's weird*, she thought. Each banana had been peeled using the monkey method. Maybe everyone already knew how to peel bananas that way!

On the bus ride to school, Amelia

Bedelia sat with her friend Joy, making plans for her zoo. "I like big cats the best," said Joy. "Where are we going to find a lion, tiger, or leopard?"

An older boy leaned over the seat behind them. "My aunt's got a really big cat," he said. "He's got tiger stripes and weighs more than thirty-seven pounds!"

"That's not big," said Amelia Bedelia. "That's enormous!"

"Yup," said the boy. "He just sits around all day, except when he waddles over to his bowl to eat."

Mrs. Shauk kept her students busy, and she kept a close eye on their work. In fact, when she taught them how animals use signals to warn one another of danger, the class took that lesson to heart. During recess, some kids figured out a way to signal everyone when the Hawk was watching. It was a matter of survival!

"We need a warning signal," said Wade.

"But it can't be too obvious or she'll catch on," said Holly.

"Well," said Teddy, "we can't slap our tails on the water like a beaver

when a coyote comes near. *Beep!*
Or whistle like prairie *Beep!*
dogs when a hawk is overhead." *Beep*

Beep-beep-beep went a truck backing up to the cafeteria to make a delivery.

They all looked at one another and got the same idea at exactly the same time. Whoever spotted the Hawk closing in would say *"Beep!"* as loudly as they dared.

When recess was over, Mrs. Shauk had the class take out their animal journals. She described different animal habitats, from rain forests and wetlands to grasslands and deserts. Amelia Bedelia tried to pay attention, but she was more interested in working on the map for her backyard, A.Z. (After Zoo).

BEEP!

It didn't take Mrs. Shauk long to catch her drawing instead of taking notes. Joy whispered, *"Beep!"* But it was too late.

"Amelia Bedelia," warned Mrs. Shauk. "I know it's fun, but you'd be better off learning about real animals in the real world instead of thinking about a zoo in your backyard. That's pie in the sky!"

Amelia Bedelia wanted to hear how a

pie could stay up in the sky, but she knew that now was not the time to ask.

At lunch, Suzanne tried to explain. "My grandma says that all the time," she said. "It's a way to say you're dreaming. She meant that your zoo isn't going to happen."

"But what does a pie in the sky have to do with animals in my backyard?" asked Amelia Bedelia.

Suzanne shrugged her shoulders and opened up her lunch box. "I don't know," she said. "But I sure hope my mom packed me some pie today!"

"Amelia Bedelia," said Heather. "We all hope you keep working on your zoo, because it's really cool. But if you hear a *beep*, watch out!"

beep!

Chapter 6

Watched Like a Shauk

After lunch, Mrs. Shauk began talking about endangered animals. Amelia Bedelia took a big risk by peeking in her notebook at the list she had made of cool animals for her zoo.

List of Animals

Angel - ball python
Roger - ~~deer head~~
Kid on bus - giant cat?
Heather - chinchilla
Joy - rabbit
Penny - mouse

She still felt bad about turning down Roger's deer head. She knew that zoologists and scientists often studied stuffed animals from long ago. Then she remembered that last year, Roger had brought a beautiful lizard for show-and-tell. It was green with gold spots and bright blue lines around its eyelids.

Amelia Bedelia made sure that Mrs. Shauk wasn't looking and wrote Roger a note.

Dear Roger,
Please bring your amazing lizard over to my house. I'll put it in my zoo. Sorry about the deer.
Amelia Bedelia

She folded the note into a tiny square,
wrote "Roger" on the outside, and passed it
to Penny . . . just as Mrs. Shauk looked up.

"*Beep!*"

beep!

Very quietly and very carefully, the
note was passed from student to student
until it reached Roger.

Mrs. Shauk was talking about polar bears
when Amelia Bedelia got her answer.

"In a few years," said Mrs. Shauk,
"polar bears might go extinct."

BEEP!

"No! I don't believe it!" blurted out Amelia Bedelia.

The entire class stared at her.

"You disagree, Amelia Bedelia?" asked Mrs. Shauk. "What if an animal disappears?"

"That's okay," said Amelia Bedelia. "If their coats or skins let them blend in, that protects them."

"You're getting ahead of us," said Mrs. Shauk. "We'll talk about natural camouflage next."

What Amelia Bedelia had not believed was the answer to her note.

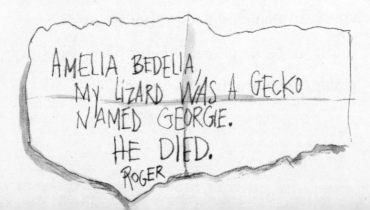

AMELIA BEDELIA,
MY LIZARD WAS A GECKO
NAMED GEORGE.
HE DIED.
ROGER

Amelia Bedelia wrote back:

When Mrs. Shauk turned toward the board, Amelia Bedelia held out the note to Penny. But Penny didn't take it. Amelia Bedelia looked at her.

"*Beep!*"

Penny was staring straight ahead, ignoring Amelia Bedelia and the note.

"*Beep!*"

Amelia Bedelia had forgotten the first rule of passing a note at school: Never take your eyes off the teacher.

"*Beep!*"

But it was too late.

Amelia Bedelia looked up at Mrs. Shauk and froze like a baby bunny in an open field. The Hawk came swooping down the aisle. Gleaming red talons plucked the note out of Amelia Bedelia's hand.

"I'll take this, young lady, and I'll see you after school."

Looking at the rest of the class, she

added, "And if I hear one more *beep* out of anyone while I am teaching, you will all join Amelia Bedelia!"

"Amelia Bedelia," Mrs. Shauk said at the end of the day. "I am so disappointed. You're usually so considerate. You pay attention. You ask good questions. Now you're drawing plans for a zoo and passing notes."

"After I missed the trip to the zoo," said Amelia Bedelia, "I just wanted to do something fun with my class and animals." Tears welled up in Amelia Bedelia's eyes.

"I see," said Mrs. Shauk. "How's it going? Are you making progress?"

Amelia Bedelia thought for a few

seconds. Then she said, "Pretty good. But it isn't easy to make an interesting zoo. Especially if you can't have the type of animals that can eat you."

Mrs. Shauk laughed and Amelia Bedelia smiled back.

"You know," said Mrs. Shauk, "I have been to lots of zoos all over the world, and I've seen thousands of animals."

"I'd love that," said Amelia Bedelia.

"It's fun to see them," said Mrs. Shauk.

"But I've always wondered what it's like to *be* them."

"That's more interesting," said Amelia Bedelia.

Mrs. Shauk nodded. "Pay more attention in class, and you might get an idea for your zoo." She handed the note back to Amelia Bedelia.

"I promise," said Amelia Bedelia.

"In my class," said Mrs. Shauk, "you can keep your head in the clouds as long as your feet are on the ground."

Getting in trouble and staying after school meant that Amelia Bedelia missed her bus, so her feet were definitely on the ground. As she waited on the bench out front for her mother to pick her up, she thought about her zoo, her friends, and what Mrs. Shauk had said.

She looked up at the sky. She could never look at clouds without seeing animals in them. Today she spotted an entire zoo overhead. A hippopotamus drifted by a rhinoceros chasing a cheetah away from a gazelle. They raced

around a huge cloud that didn't have much shape. It was rounded on top and flat on the bottom, like a giant tortoise with its head and legs tucked inside its shell—no, wait a second. . . .

Amelia Bedelia couldn't believe it. It was a pie! A pie in the sky! She pointed at it, but no one was around to share it with her. Suddenly it changed into a lizard and scampered away.

"If there can be a pie in the sky," Amelia Bedelia said, "then there can be a zoo in my backyard!"

Chapter 7

Leapin' Lizards — a Glacial Gecko!

When Amelia Bedelia finally got home, Roger was already waiting. Sitting on the doorstep next to him was a plastic cooler.

"You didn't have to bring your own refreshments," said Amelia Bedelia. "We have cold drinks."

"Amelia Bedelia's right," said her mother, laughing. "I'll go make you some lemonade."

Roger stared at Amelia Bedelia and patted the top of the cooler. "Georgie is in here," he whispered.

Amelia Bedelia felt creeped out . . . and curious. Why would Roger bring a dead gecko over to her house?

"Don't worry," said Roger. "Georgie doesn't stink. He's frozen solid."

Then he told Amelia Bedelia how his little brother had let Georgie out of his terrarium to show to some friends. Georgie had disappeared, and they found him flattened under a sofa cushion. It was winter, and the ground was too frozen to bury him. So they put him in a plastic bag and stuck him in the freezer until the ground thawed and he could have a proper burial.

"Georgie died five months ago," said Roger. "I had pretty much forgotten about him until I got your note. Would you like to see him?"

Amelia Bedelia nodded, so Roger opened the cooler, pushed aside an ice pack, and held up the gecko. Georgie was in a plastic bag. He was flattened out like he had been run over.

Amelia Bedelia was fascinated. She didn't notice Clay coming up the walk. "Cool!" he said. "What's that?"

"It's more than cool," said Amelia Bedelia. "It's frozen."

"It's Georgie," said Roger. "I never got a chance to bury him. He's a gold dust day gecko from Madagascar."

Amelia Bedelia didn't know what to do. She had imagined having a zoo, not a museum.

"This is amazing," said Clay. "We can make a sign that says he's a reptile and that even though the word dinosaur means 'terrible lizard,' he's not a dinosaur. We can say Georgie is an ancient lizard that fell into a glacier and was perfectly preserved to this very day."

"We can write that he liked to eat all kinds of insects and bugs," said Roger.

"Even the flu?" asked Amelia Bedelia. "Because that would be great."

"Let's freeze him in a block of ice," said Clay. "He'll be the main attraction!"

"I'll put him in our

birdbath," said Amelia Bedelia. She was beginning to see the possibilities in this idea. "Georgie will be on a pedestal, and it can hold the melting water."

Roger looked relieved. "Once he thaws out, we can bury him."

"Absolutely," said Amelia Bedelia.

Amelia Bedelia, Clay, and Roger sneaked Georgie into the kitchen. They were about to fill the plastic bag with water when they heard Amelia Bedelia's mother coming. They resealed it and tucked it into the back of the freezer, behind a bag of frozen peas.

That night, everything for dinner was fresh, so the freezer door stayed shut. Amelia Bedelia had already told her mother why she had to stay late at school, but during dessert she told her father too.

"You want to build a zoo?" asked her father. "With real animals?"

"Just pets," she replied. "Like Finally . . . and Joy has a rabbit and Penny has a mouse. Lots of kids in my class have pets. Plus we'll probably use some stuffed animals."

"You started to tell me this the other day, didn't you? So *that's* why that snake was in our backyard!" said her mother.

"A snake! In our backyard?" said

Amelia Bedelia's father. "Forget it!"

"Oh, Daddy, please?" said Amelia Bedelia. "It's a really Big Idea. We'll have games and rides too."

"Sweetie," he said, "building a zoo is complicated. It would be different if you'd done some planning."

Amelia Bedelia excused herself and ran to her bedroom. She returned with her notebook. She showed her parents the plan for her zoo. It included everything, from the rope-swing entrance to the birdbath glacier display. All of the animals and exhibits were organized into habitats.

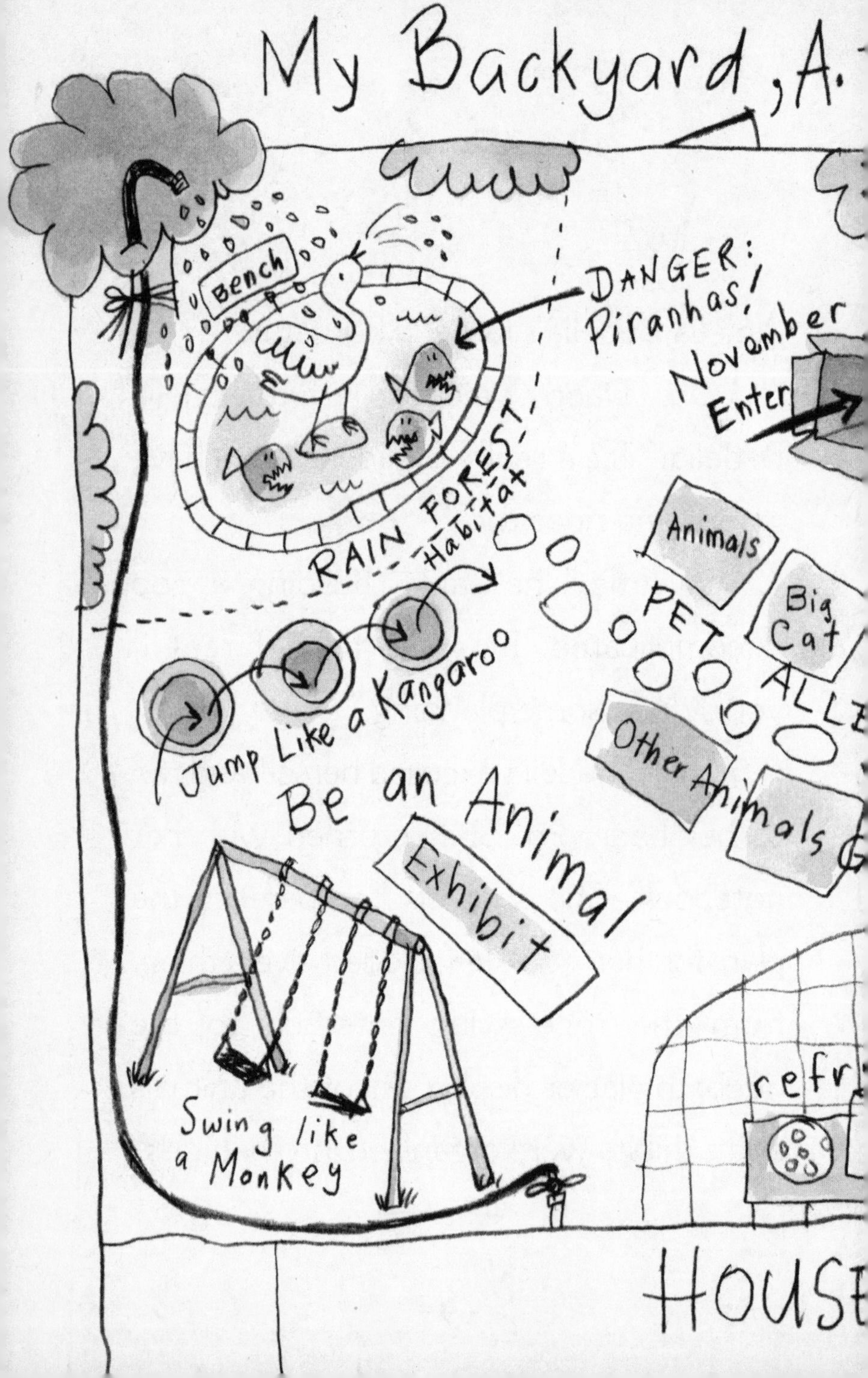

My Backyard, A.

bench

DANGER:
Piranhas!

November
Enter

RAIN FOREST
Habitat

Jump Like a Kangaroo

Be an Animal

Exhibit

Swing like
a Monkey

Animals

Big
Cat

PET
ALLE

Other Animals

refr

HOUSE

(After Zoo) ☺

Vegetable

April Exit

Georgie

ibernation
unnel

Garden

Garage

als

Rope
Swing

nts

Enter
here

Amelia Bedelia's parents looked at the map, at each other, and then at Amelia Bedelia. "So," said her father, smiling, "when I fell into your wading pool, it was actually a crocodile-infested river?"

"Uh-huh," said Amelia Bedelia. "Sorry."

"And my herb garden will be home to a Big Cat?" asked her mother.

"Yup. But it never moves," said Amelia Bedelia. "It won't bother anything."

Her father shrugged. "Looks harmless enough, I suppose."

"And you did a great job of planning," said her mother. "Let us sleep on it, and we'll let you know in the morning."

Amelia Bedelia handed her notebook to her mother. "Just don't sleep on it too much," she said. "If it gets wrinkled, I'll have to do it over."

Amelia Bedelia put on her pajamas and kissed her parents good-night. She lay in bed looking at the sweet squirrel monkey perched on her windowsill. She loved her gift, and she felt really lucky to have such

good friends at school. She could just see
the reflection of the monkey in the glass.
Two monkeys are better than one, she
thought.

She was about to turn off her lamp

when she noticed that her monkey had lost his reflection. *That's odd,* she thought. Then Amelia Bedelia's own animal instinct kicked in.

She got out of bed and rummaged through her backpack. Where was that extra banana her mother always packed? Got it! She raised her window and set the banana on the ledge.

Leaves rustled in a nearby tree as she closed the window. Back in bed, Amelia Bedelia whispered, "Good night, little monkey."

Chapter 8

Pet Peeved

Amelia Bedelia checked her windowsill as soon as she got up the next morning. The banana was gone! She raced downstairs and ran outside to look for the peel. There it was! She picked it up so that her father wouldn't slip again. She was so excited, she didn't know what to do. The banana had been peeled exactly the same way

the monkeys had peeled their
bananas on the TV show.

At breakfast, Amelia Bedelia's mother
and father told her that it was okay for her
to build her zoo as long as one of them was
at home and as long as everyone helping had
permission to be at Amelia Bedelia's house.
Also, no dangerous pets were allowed.

"That's great!" said Amelia Bedelia.
"Mom, will you get me more bananas,
please—like a big bunch of bananas?"

"*More* bananas?" said her mother.
"You already eat two a day."

"She may look like Amelia Bedelia," said
her father. "But she's actually the monkey
that escaped from the zoo. Do you know,
they still haven't caught that little fella!"

Amelia Bedelia froze, like prey caught in the open. Had her dad guessed what she was thinking? Did her dad know something she didn't know? Then she remembered her Rule #1: If you don't know what to say, ask a question.

"Dad, do you know how a monkey eats a banana?" she asked.

"With relish," said her father.

"Yuck!" said Amelia Bedelia. "A banana with relish would taste terrible. Save it for your hot dog!"

Amelia Bedelia grabbed a banana from the fruit bowl and showed her dad how to peel it using the Monkey Method.

"Amazing,"

said her father. "Who knew?" He cut up the banana and put it on his cereal.

"I was thinking," said Amelia Bedelia, "that I could offer my friends bananas for a snack this afternoon. They're healthy."

"I'm glad to hear you say that," said Amelia Bedelia's mother. "I'll get you a bunch of bunches."

And that is how Amelia Bedelia's Rule #2 was born: Include the word "healthy" in your request or comment, and grown-ups will automatically agree.

That afternoon after school, Amelia Bedelia and her friends worked on Pet Alley and the Rain Forest Habitat. They made signs and installed the hose

RAIN FOREST

in the apple tree. They got a ton done. But too soon it was time for everyone to go home to do their homework. Amelia Bedelia was just heading upstairs when she heard a commotion in the kitchen. It was her father, and he was not happy. He was holding something behind his back.

"Young lady," her father began. (This was not a good sign, in Amelia Bedelia's experience.) "I was searching for an after-work, before-dinner treat. I had my heart set on ice cream. A morsel of rocky road, perhaps. Instead I find . . . roadkill lizard!" He held up a plastic bag of frozen gecko.

"That's Georgie," said Amelia Bedelia. "A gold dust day gecko from Madagascar."

"I don't care if it's Robin Hood from Sherwood Forest," said her father. "He doesn't belong in our freezer. What if your mother had found this thing?"

"I forgot he was in there," said Amelia Bedelia. "I need him for my zoo."

"Zoo!" bellowed her father. "This poor creature is frozen stiff!"

Amelia Bedelia explained everything, including Clay's idea to freeze Georgie in a block of ice that would be placed on the birdbath pedestal. Amelia Bedelia's father

81

shook his head, then smiled. He glanced out the window at the driveway.

"We don't have much time," he said. "Mom just went to run a quick errand, and she'll be back any second."

They made a good team. Amelia Bedelia's dad acted like a surgeon performing a delicate operation, and Amelia Bedelia was his nurse.

"Milk carton," he said.

Amelia Bedelia handed him a large carton of milk from the refrigerator, and he poured the milk into a pitcher. Then he opened the carton at the top, sponged it out, and held it under the faucet.

"Water," he said.

Amelia Bedelia turned on the faucet

and filled the carton with water.

"Lizard," he said.

"Gecko," said Amelia Bedelia, correcting him as she handed him Georgie in his plastic bag.

"Oh, no," said her dad. "This is your zoo. You do the honors."

Amelia Bedelia made a face as she looked at her father and then at the flattened, frozen gecko in the bag. She sighed, then opened the bag and extracted Georgie by his tail. She lowered him into the milk carton, headfirst. Georgie fit perfectly.

"Tape," said her dad. He closed up the end of the milk carton and taped it shut.

Then he buried it in the back of the freezer.

"I hid him behind a frozen chunk of your grandmother's fruitcake," he said. "That would frighten off anyone."

Amelia Bedelia agreed. "Her fruitcake is scarier than a dead lizard."

"Gecko," said her father, correcting her.

Just then the back door swung open. Amelia Bedelia's mother came in carrying groceries.

"What's that pitcher of milk doing on the counter?" she asked.

"The carton was leaking," fibbed Amelia Bedelia's father.

"Dad notices all kinds of things," said Amelia Bedelia.

Her father winked at her.

Amelia Bedelia winked back.

Amelia Bedelia's mother started unpacking the groceries. "Honey, I half expected to catch you sneaking a bowl of rocky road ice cream when I came in," she said.

"Sweetheart," he said, "I'm shocked you'd think that!"

"Sorry," she said, giving Amelia Bedelia's father a hug. "Good news! Lamb chops were on sale."

"Oh, they're my favorite!" he said.

While her parents were discussing recipes, Amelia Bedelia reached into the fruit bowl and broke off three bananas. Hiding them behind her, she backed out of the kitchen. She didn't give those lamb chops a second thought. If she had, she would have realized they were *baaaaaaa*-d news.

Chapter 9
Monkey shines

That evening, after she had eaten dinner and finished all of her homework, Amelia Bedelia grabbed her three bananas and went out to the backyard. Her brain hurt from too much thinking. She still couldn't hear herself think, but she could definitely feel it. She was thinking like Amelia Bedelia and trying to think like a monkey

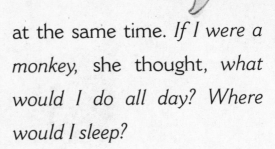

at the same time. *If I were a monkey,* she thought, *what would I do all day? Where would I sleep?*

She went into her garage to look for something that might catch a monkey. If she could actually capture a real, live monkey, her zoo would be the best ever. She found a long, skinny net, but that was for their badminton set. She found boxes, some garden stakes, and a spool of string. Next to a croquet set, she discovered a relic from her past—her car seat.

Amelia Bedelia sat down in it. She was way too big for it now, so it was a tight squeeze, but she fit. There was a harness, a snack holder, and a cup holder. She

Beep! Beep! remembered that she hadn't liked riding in it until her dad installed a horn in the snack holder. *Beep-beep!* It still worked. Amazing. She used to drive her mother crazy, beeping at every car she saw.

If I were a monkey, I would sit right here, thought Amelia Bedelia. *It would be my recliner—just like Dad's. I'd take naps in it.* She put one of the bananas in the seat. She peeled another banana and left a trail of pieces from the side door of the garage to the tree near her bedroom window. Then she went inside to get ready for bed.

Amelia Bedelia brushed her teeth and put on her pajamas and kissed her parents good-night. Then she read two chapters in her book. She was just about to turn off the light when she remembered to put a banana on the ledge outside her window. She nudged her stuffed squirrel monkey to the side and was just opening the window when a face popped up on the other side of the glass.

"Yahhhhhhh!" screamed Amelia Bedelia, flinging the banana and her stuffed monkey into the air.

Seconds later, her mother and father ran into her room.

"What's wrong?" asked her mother.

"I saw something!" said Amelia Bedelia. She sat on the bed hugging her mother while her father looked out the window, in the closet, and under the bed.

"The only thing I found is this banana,"
he said, his shirt covered with dust bunnies.

Amelia Bedelia was still shaking. "I—I
saw something moving outside," she said.

Her father picked up the toy monkey and handed it to her. "Bitty baby baboon," he said, "you've been eating too many bananas. Did you mistake this for a real monkey?"

Amelia Bedelia's mother laughed and tucked in Amelia Bedelia and her monkey. "Good night, sweetie," she said, "and good night, little imp."

As soon as her parents turned off the light and closed her door, Amelia Bedelia slipped out of bed and looked out the window. She hoped she hadn't scared the real monkey away. The moon was shining brightly down on the backyard zoo. She looked to the right and then to the left.

Right there! A real, live monkey was

scampering on top of the garage and eating a banana. She almost yelled, "Yippee!" but her parents would have come running again, and she wasn't ready to explain her plan to them. She hoped the monkey would discover her old car seat. She hoped he would be cozy in his recliner all night, dreaming of the tropical forest.

Chapter 10

Monkey Saw, Monkey Did

The next day was unusual—there were no catastrophes. In school, Amelia Bedelia focused on learning all about monkeys. Mrs. Shauk was happy to see her paying attention again.

Amelia Bedelia's friend Pat was really handy at building things. Pat's dad also had tons of tools, so during recess, she asked Pat if he could borrow some tools and rig up something special for her. That afternoon, while everyone else was working on the exhibits, Amelia Bedelia took Pat to the garage to show him what she wanted, but she did not tell him exactly why she wanted it.

Amelia Bedelia had researched how to train a monkey. She had learned that monkeys are very clever and can be taught to do amazing things. Monkeys had even flown into space, and they could assist people who needed help with everyday things. For example, if you dropped your keys and couldn't reach them yourself, you could teach your monkey to pick them up.

The best way to train a monkey was to show it how to do something and let it copy you—monkey see, monkey do. Of course, using a treat as a reward helped. Amelia Bedelia felt the same way. She would do almost anything for a double-fudge brownie.

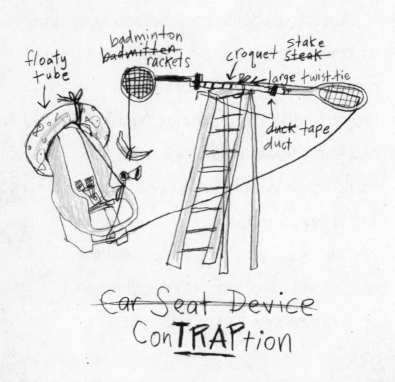

floaty tube

badminton
~~badmitten~~
rackets

croquet ~~stake~~ steak

large twist-tie

~~duck~~ tape
duct

~~Car Seat Device~~
ConTRAPtion

Together, Amelia Bedelia
and Pat drew up a plan.

"This is definitely a
contraption," said Pat.

Amelia Bedelia liked that word. She
wrote it on a big piece of poster board
while Pat worked. She opened up cans of
her dad's old paint and made some signs for
her zoo.

Her favorite was:

MRS. SHAUK SAYS,

BE AN ANIMAL!

When she had
painted all the signs she could think of and
Pat was still working on the contraption,
she decided to tour the backyard to check
on everyone's progress.

Dawn was putting the final
touches on a giant pair of ears.
"Here, try them!" she said.
Amelia Bedelia put them on while
Dawn walked to the edge of the yard
and whispered a question to
test them.

"Wow," said Amelia Bedelia.
"Yes, I can hear just like
a jackrabbit!"

Then she tried on a
pair of fuzzy slippers
next to the rodent display.
They let her walk as quietly
as a mouse. A pair of
binoculars would let visitors
see like a hawk (or a Shauk).

Chip and Heather were finishing up the hibernation tunnel. At the entrance, they had taped a sign that said NOVEMBER and at the exit there was a sign that said APRIL. When the flaps at both ends of the tunnel were shut, it was pitch dark inside. There were pillows and blankets and a window inside the tunnel, but when the curtains were pushed aside, the "hibernator" just saw snow flurries!

Amelia Bedelia made a list of hibernating animals in her notebook. They

were so amazing! She had most of these animals—except maybe a hedgehog—in the stuffed-animal basket in her room. Joy probably had a stuffed hedgehog, she thought. They could tuck all the animals under the blankets in the tunnel!

Soon it was almost time for supper. Amelia Bedelia's friends left one by one. Just before he went home, Pat installed the dangling banana. Amelia Bedelia sat down in the car seat and pulled the banana

to her. She did it a couple of times, hoping
that she was teaching someone. Unknown
to her, monkey eyes were watching.

The next morning, the car-seat banana
was missing. "So far, so good," said Amelia
Bedelia. "Monkey saw, monkey did."

Chapter 11

A Sheep in Sheep's Clothing

Finally it was Friday, the last day before the zoo was to officially open. Everyone in Amelia Bedelia's class came to her house after school to make sure that the zoo would be ready in time.

Pat and Amelia Bedelia went straight to the garage to work on the contraption. They tested it a couple of times. It took

three seconds after the treat was grabbed for the inflatable tube to fall into place. All that was missing was a banana . . . and a monkey.

Rose's mother stopped by with cupcakes for everyone and three mini trampolines! Amelia Bedelia and Rose decided to set them up in a line, one right after the other. Rose hopped on. *Boing-boing-boing!*

"I'm a kangaroo!" she hollered.

Then everyone had to try it.

The trampolines were the perfect addition to the Be an Animal! exhibit.

marks on a tree from a BEAR

hole made by a WOODPECKER

marks from a BEAVER

The whole class worked together on the final exhibit—Signs of Animals. There was a section of a tree trunk with claw marks made from clay. It looked exactly like a bear had been there! Penny used more clay on another tree to make it look like a beaver had gnawed the wood. And Nate used a dark brown marker to create fake holes—a woodpecker searching for bugs!

That night, Amelia Bedelia's family sat down to a special dinner of grilled lamb chops. Her father had been talking about dinner nonstop since he came home from work. At last, the table was set, the candles were lit, and dinner was served. "Mmmmm," he said. *Baaaaa*

"Baaaaaaa."

Amelia Bedelia's father looked at Amelia Bedelia's mother, who looked at Amelia Bedelia, who tried to look like nothing had happened. Amelia Bedelia's father shrugged and popped a bite of lamb into his mouth. *baaaa-baaaa!*

"Baaaaaaaaa!"

Amelia Bedelia's dad stopped chewing. "Sweetheart," he said, "either this is the freshest lamb you've ever made, or there is a sheep right outside our window."

They both looked at Amelia Bedelia.

"You look sheepish," said her mother.

Baaaaa-baaaa-baaaa!

"Sheepish?" said Amelia Bedelia. "I'm not a sheep. What sheep?"

"Baaaaa, baaaaaa, baaaaaa!"

Her parents jumped up and ran outside, with Amelia Bedelia close behind them. The sun was setting, songbirds were chirping, and a sheep was grazing on the grass. This peaceful scene lasted less than a second.

"Okay, young lady," said her mother. "Out with it. What's that sheep doing in our yard?"

"Ummm . . . eating supper?" said Amelia Bedelia.

Amelia Bedelia's mother put her hands on her hips, her eyes narrowing to slits.

Amelia Bedelia's father gazed up at the
heavens as he slowly shook his head.

Amelia Bedelia realized that she had
run out of luck. It was time for the truth.

"You know Wade, right? Well, Wade's

Baaaaa

uncle, Fred, has a farm," she explained. "He grows vegetables and he has animals like chickens and pigs and sheep and cows. When he came to town today for the farmer's market, he dropped off a spare sheep."

"Sweetie," said Amelia Bedelia's mother. "I don't recall giving you permission to have a sheep."

"But my zoo opens tomorrow," said Amelia Bedelia. "Uncle Fred will stop by afterward and pick it up."

"Look," said her father. "Your ideas are super, but you've gone wild! You're making me nuts with these animals. Are you trying to get my goat?"

"Goat?" said Amelia Bedelia. "If I knew you had a goat, I wouldn't have gotten a sheep."

Amelia Bedelia's mother clapped her hand to her mouth and snorted. "Amelia Bedelia," she said, trying not to laugh, "you don't have any more animals up your sleeve, do you?"

"See for yourselves," said Amelia Bedelia, rolling up both of her sleeves. "Empty!"

Now her father was trying not to laugh. But he managed to say, "No more surprise animals, young lady!" in his firmest

I'm-really-not-kidding-this-time voice.

"Cross my heart," said Amelia Bedelia, tracing a giant X on her chest.

Luckily the sheep was wearing a collar. Amelia Bedelia's father tied a rope to the collar and led the sheep to a spot where it would have plenty of grass but couldn't reach any of her mother's flower beds.

"I need to attach the rope to something," he said. "Any ideas?"

"How about a stake?" asked Amelia Bedelia's mother.

"Dad doesn't need a steak," said Amelia Bedelia. "He's got a plate full of lamb chops waiting for him."

Baaaaaa

Her parents looked at her, then at each other, and then at the sheep.

"Baaaaaaaaa!"

"Here's an idea," said Amelia Bedelia's father. "Let's put those lamb chops in the fridge. I vote we all go out for pizza. All those in favor, say baaaaaaaaa!" *baa*

"Baaaaaaaaa!" said Amelia Bedelia.

"Baaaaaaaaa!" said her mother.

"Baaaaaaaaa!" said the sheep.

"It's ewe-nanimous!" said her father.

Baaaaaa   *Baaaaa*

ewe (noun): a female sheep

"Hey, Mom and Dad," Amelia Bedelia said from the backseat as they pulled out of the driveway. "When we get back home, remind me to call and cancel the cow."

Now she was the one who couldn't keep a straight face. She burst out laughing and her parents did too, and they laughed all the way to the Perfect Pizza Parlor.

Chapter 12

Getting Skunked Twice

Late that night, Finally began acting very strangely. She danced at the back door, whining, growling, and barking.

Amelia Bedelia's father opened the door from the outside—he had just put out the trash—and Finally tore past him and ran into the backyard.

"Wow," said Amelia Bedelia's father.

BARK BARK!

"I'd hate to run into Finally! She's loaded for bear."

"Daddy, what are you talking about?" said Amelia Bedelia. "We don't have any bears in our backyard! Only a sheep."

Finally barked, then growled, then yelped.

"Whoa!" said Amelia Bedelia's father. "Do you smell that?"

Anyone with a nose could smell that. Finally had been sprayed by a skunk!

"No chance," said Amelia Bedelia's father when Finally appeared at the back door, eager to come in. "You raised a stink, and then you found one. We need to clean you up first."

Amelia Bedelia's mother called Diana

the dog walker to ask for a recipe for getting rid of the skunk odor. Luckily, Finally got more of a skunk spritz than a full spray. Amelia Bedelia and her parents took turns scrubbing, so she cleaned up pretty quickly. The only good part was that before they scrubbed her, Amelia Bedelia took a clipping of Finally's hair and put it in a plastic bag. She wrote SKUNK SMELL on the outside of the bag. She'd add it to the Signs of Animals exhibit in the morning, with a warning to anyone brave enough to take a whiff.

It was getting late. Amelia Bedelia couldn't wait for tomorrow. She grabbed a banana from the fruit bowl and was heading out to the garage when her mother stopped her.

"Where are you going? You're not leaving the house with a skunk loose in our backyard—and it's time for bed!"

"Hey," said her father. "Did you invite that skunk to your zoo?"

Amelia Bedelia would have smiled, but she was upset that she couldn't put a banana in the car-seat contraption for the monkey. All that work! All those plans! She trudged upstairs and left the banana on her windowsill, as usual. She had really wanted to catch that monkey for her zoo. Just like Finally, Amelia Bedelia had been skunked.

Chapter 13

More Fun Than a Barrel of Monkeys

Everything was set for the grand opening of Amelia Bedelia's zoo. The rope swing was ready, pets were displayed on tables, the sheep was happily eating the lawn, and kids were waiting to guide visitors through the exhibits.

Georgie looked fantastic on the birdbath. Tiny gold flecks on his bright

green skin glittered through the ice. Even the thin turquoise line around his eyelids shone brightly. His claws were just beginning to poke out.

Amelia Bedelia had one last thing to do.

She got a banana and went to the garage. She tied the banana to the contraption and sighed. The zoo was already getting noisy. Too noisy for a squirrel monkey. Maybe the monkey would come tonight, when things quieted down.

Everyone loved the zoo. While the Big Cat was sitting as still as a statue on her enormous pillow, other pets were showing off and doing tricks. Visitors loved jumping like kangaroos. The hibernation tunnel was a huge hit. And Amelia Bedelia knew the zoo was a success when she saw Mrs. Shauk swing

across the wading pool and land in her backyard.

"Amelia Bedelia," Mrs. Shauk said, "your backyard looks like more fun than a barrel of monkeys!"

"Monkeys are the last thing we need," said Amelia Bedelia's father.

BEEP! BEEP! BEEP!

BEEP! BEEP!

They were all laughing when . . .

Beep!

Amelia Bedelia could tell that Mrs. Shauk was not amused.

Beep! Beep!

But she couldn't figure out who was beeping.

Beep! Beep! Beep!

"Wow," said Amelia Bedelia's mother, "I haven't heard that sound since you were little."

Amelia Bedelia's heart began racing.

Beep! Beep! Beep!

"It's coming from the garage," said her father.

Everyone raced to the garage.

Beep! Beep!

On the floor of the garage was Amelia Bedelia's car seat. Sitting happily in the car seat, munching a banana and pushing the toy horn, was the cutest squirrel monkey ever.

Beeeeeeeeep!

BEEP
BEEP

Chapter 14

Monkey Business

Amelia Bedelia's father called the zoo immediately to let them know that their lost monkey had been found. Her mother and Mrs. Shauk kept the other kids back while Amelia Bedelia baby-stepped toward it, banana in hand.

"He's happy as long as he's eating bananas," said Amelia Bedelia.

Her mother raced to the kitchen and brought back every banana they had.

In minutes, a team from the zoo rushed into the driveway carrying nets and a travel crate. When they saw their

monkey in a car seat, happily munching on a banana, they relaxed a bit. The television news team arrived soon after that, and then the director of the city zoo. Amelia Bedelia posed with both monkeys, the real one and the one from the gift shop. Then she handed a banana to the real monkey, and everyone saw how he peeled it.

The news team interviewed Amelia Bedelia and her friends, filmed their pets, and toured the exhibits. A reporter interviewed the zoo director about the backyard zoo and Mrs. Shauk about all of the great things her students had done.

"I love these Be an Animal exhibits," said the director. "This is just what our zoo needs!" He invited Mrs. Shauk and her class back to the zoo to talk about their ideas.

BEEP! BEEP!

Mrs. Shauk turned to Amelia Bedelia. "Here is the person with the big imagination," she said. "Congratulations, Amelia Bedelia. I will have to eat crow."

"Please don't," said Amelia Bedelia. "I'd rather have a crow in my zoo than in your stomach."

Finally it was time to take the monkey back to the zoo. Amelia Bedelia sat down beside him and gave him one last banana. He peeled it in a flash. But instead of gobbling it down, he offered it to her.

"Thanks," she said. "For everything."
She patted him on the top of his head. It
felt warm, and his hair was wiry, not like
her toy monkey at all.

"Good night, little monkey," she said.

Beep! Beep!

beep!

BEEP!

Chapter 15

Grim and Bear It

Amelia Bedelia couldn't believe it. She had returned a missing monkey to the real zoo; she had created, with all of her friends, a great backyard zoo; and her teacher had actually liked it! But now it was all over. As people began leaving, Roger came up to her.

"Georgie's almost defrosted," he said.

"Can we have his funeral now?"

"Sure," said Amelia Bedelia. "You can take him home."

"Can we bury him in your backyard?" said Roger. "Georgie likes it here."

Amelia Bedelia understood. She got a trowel from the garage and dug a good-sized hole—so that what was left of the block of ice would fit—next to an azalea bush.

"We'll put a mound of dirt on top and plant some flowers," she said.

Roger nodded. "Amelia Bedelia," he said, "would you please say a few words about Georgie?"

Amelia Bedelia did not expect that. Georgie hadn't been her pet. But then she

thought, *Why not?* After learning about animals, thinking like a monkey, and building a zoo, Amelia Bedelia was pretty qualified. The only thing that bothered

her was that after all the fun they had had, now they were having a funeral. But Roger was her friend. She shrugged and said what her grandmother always said: "Ah well, that's life."

Everyone who was still in Amelia Bedelia's backyard—kids and parents and pets—gathered around. Amelia Bedelia cleared her throat and began.

"Roger's pet gecko, Georgie, came from Madagascar. It's a big island next to Africa, so Georgie was far from home when he passed away. He was little, but he was an amazing, colorful, complicated animal. Roger really loved him, and when he died, Roger kept Georgie in a cold, dark place until he could give him a funeral like he deserved. But first, Georgie spent today teaching kids about animals. Now he's ready to rest. I'll plant forget-me-not flowers on top of you, because none of us will ever forget you, Georgie."

Amelia Bedelia turned to Roger, who was holding the block of ice. Then Roger did another thing that Amelia Bedelia had not expected. He gave Georgie a kiss. No one looked away or squirmed or thought *Eewwww—Roger just kissed a dead lizard!*

No, this was a last kiss good-bye, good-bye and thank you, good-bye forever, my friend.

Some kids began to sniffle. Some grown-up eyes glistened. Even people who had never had a pet were moved by what Amelia Bedelia had said. What was true for Georgie was true for all animals—they were all amazing miracles, just like Georgie had been.

There was nothing left to say, but no one felt like leaving, either. Everybody just wanted to stay right there, next to one another.

Amelia Bedelia's mother gave her a hug. "Nice job, sweetie. I'll go get some snacks. Your friends can hang out here until the cows come home."

"MOOOOOO!"

A truck was backing into the driveway. The sides were painted with fruits and vegetables and a sign that read UNCLE FRED'S FARM.

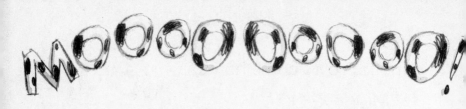

"MOOOOOOOOOOOOOOO!"

A cow gazed down at them.

"MOOOOOOOOOOOOOOOO!"

Amelia Bedelia's father ran up to her and loudly whispered, "I thought you were kidding about canceling the cow!"

"I was," said Amelia Bedelia. "I didn't order a cow!"

Wade's uncle Fred got out of the truck and introduced himself. "Just stopped by to pick up my nephew and my sheep," he said. "I can loan you Gertrude here, if you'd like to have a cow."

"That won't be necessary," said Amelia Bedelia's mother. "My husband

140

has had a cow every day this week."

Uncle Fred chuckled. Amelia Bedelia had no idea what her mother meant. She figured that her father's cows must be with his goat.

As Uncle Fred loaded the sheep into his truck, Amelia Bedelia's father said, "I'll miss that fuzzy lawn mower. Now I have to mow the grass again."

That night, after supper, Amelia Bedelia and her parents sat outside on the patio with Finally, who still smelled a little bit like skunk.

Looking out over their backyard, they recalled all the fun and excitement of the zoo and the days leading up it.

"Amelia Bedelia," asked her mother. "I just have one question. Why is there a banana on your windowsill?"

Amelia Bedelia laughed. She laughed so hard that she could not stop. Soon her parents were laughing too.

"That was a wild time," said Amelia Bedelia's father.

"I already miss it," said her mother.

"You do?" said Amelia Bedelia.

"Me too," said her father. "I told the director how you didn't get to go on the field trip to the zoo. We're meeting him tomorrow morning. He's taking the three of us on a VIP tour."

Amelia Bedelia jumped up and yelled, "Thank you, Daddy! Family hug!"

It was their wildest family hug ever.

Squirrel Monkeys

Squirrel monkeys live in t[he] rain forests of Central Americ[a] South America. They live in th[e] canopy of the forest. That means a top of the trees. They mostly ea[t] insects and fruits (like bananas[)]

Ball Pythons

Ball pythons are from Afr[ica] They don't have any venum venom. These snakes fold into a ball shape when they thi[nk] something is going to attac[k] them. You can **ROLL** a ball python. They eat mice.

Hawks

Hawks are birds of prey. That means they eat other animals and birds. There are all kinds of ha[wks] (red-tailed hawks, sharp-shinned hawks, sparrow hawks, and more). They have **REALLY** good eyesight.

Mice

There are field mice and house mice and they are all SOOOO CUTE! Mice are rodents. They can be really great pets. ♡

Sheep

A boy sheep is a **RAM**, a girl sheep is a **EWE**, and a baby sheep is called a **LAMB**. A sheep's hair is called **WOOL** and people use it to make clothes. Sheep live almost all over the world and appear in stories and tales and rhymes, such as "Baa, baa, black sheep."

Skunks

Did you know that skunks are also called polecats? Their spray is super stinky and they spray when they sense danger nearby, like a dog or bear. Baby skunks are called **kits**.

gold dust day geckos

These lizards are from the island of MADAGASCAR. They eat insects and also drink nectar from plants and flowers. If their tails fall off, they can grow new ones! ☺

Read all these great books about Amelia Bedelia!

Amelia Bedelia Means Business

#1

by Herman Parish pictures by Lynne Avril

Amelia Bedelia Unleashed

#2

by Herman Parish pictures by Lynne Avril

Amelia Bedelia Road Trip!

WRONG WAY ADVENTURE

RIGHT WAY

#3

by H... pictures by Lynne Avril

Amelia Bedelia Goes Wild!

#4

by Herman Parish pictures by Lynne Avril

Amelia Bedelia

Hi!
Turn the page
for a special
sneak peek
at my next
adventure!

#5

Amelia
Bedelia

#5

Shapes Up

by Herman Parish   pictures by Lynne Avril

Coming soon!

Chapter 1

Heads Up!

Amelia Bedelia did not wake up one morning and say to herself, "What a beautiful day! I can't wait for all my friends to laugh at me."

But she might as well have, because that is just what happened.

One good thing was that it really *was* a beautiful day. After studying

math all morning, everyone was ready for recess . . . except Mrs. Robbins.

"Amelia Bedelia," said Mrs. Robbins, "what if I gave you a pie . . ."

"Thank you," said Amelia Bedelia. "I love pie."

"I'm not really giving you a pie," said Mrs. Robbins. "Let's pretend."

Two Ways to Say It

By Amelia Bedelia

"I'm sick as a dog."  "I'm really, really sick."

"That's a pie in the sky idea!" "That's a great idea, but it will never happen."

"Your head is in the clouds!" "You are so busy daydreaming, you don't know what's going on!"

"His sweater is covered with dust bunnies." "His sweater is covered with fluffy bits of dust."

"You look sheepish." "You look a bit embarrassed."

"Are you trying to get my goat?" "Are you trying to upset me?"